© 1995 Tormont Publications Inc., 338 St. Antoine Street East, Montreal, Quebec, Canada H2Y 1A3, Tel.: (514) 954-1441, Fax: (514) 954-5086
Illustrations: Zapp Graphic Design: Zapp Text: Carol Krenz
ISBN 2-89429-618-5 Printed in U.S.A.

Snow White

ONCE upon a time, there lived a gentle Queen who longed for a daughter. One day, as she sat by an open window stitching embroidery in her ebony hoop, she was so distracted by her secret wish that she pricked a finger with her sewing needle.

Little drops of blood fell onto the fresh snow on the window ledge. She looked at the bright scarlet against the pure white and sighed. "How lovely it would be to have a daughter with skin as white as snow, lips as red as blood and hair as dark as ebony!" she whispered to herself.

It wasn't long before her wish came true. Her baby daughter had pale skin, rose-red lips and hair as black as ebony. The Queen named her Snow White.

But the Queen soon died, and Snow White's father married another woman, cruel and beautiful, who worried more about her looks than kind deeds.

THE WICKED Queen owned a magic mirror that could answer any question at all. But the only question the Queen ever asked was:

"Mirror, mirror on the wall, Who is the fairest one of all?"

The mirror always replied:

"You, great Queen, are the fairest to be seen!"

Well, the Queen was very pleased until one day, the Mirror said something entirely different:

"It's true your Majesty is regal and grand.

But Snow White is the fairest in all the land."

THE WICKED Queen choked on her rage and jealousy. Snow White more beautiful than she? Never! She simply would not allow it. So she called for her huntsman.

"Take Snow White out into the forest and kill her!" the Queen commanded. "And bring back her heart to me as proof."

The huntsman bowed his head in obedience and searched the castle for Snow White.

"Where are we going?" asked Snow White.

"A picnic in the woods, your Highness," replied the huntsman.

But his heart was heavy and he knew he could never kill the innocent princess. So, once in the forest, he told Snow White about the Queen's jealous rage. "Run away from here," he advised. "Hide in the woods and don't try to come back to the palace!"

Snow White cried with fear and ran deep into the forest. Meanwhile, the huntsman killed a wild boar in the bushes and took its heart back to the palace.

"The Queen will think this belongs to Snow White," he thought. "The princess and I will live a little while longer."

SNOW WHITE was terrified in the woods. It was very dark, and often she tripped over snake-like vines.

She wandered about for hours, lost and cold, until at last she saw a tiny cottage. It was so cleverly built out of a large tree stump that she nearly walked right past it.

"IS ANYONE home?" she called, as she knocked loudly at the little door. It swung open and she stepped inside to discover a tidy room with a round table and seven stools.

Feeling safe and warm, Snow White climbed a staircase to a loft where she saw seven small beds all in a row.

"Perhaps I can take a short nap," she thought. "I'm so very sleepy."

She lay down and stretched across the beds. Soon she fell into an exhausted sleep.

THAT evening, the Seven Dwarfs who owned the little house returned home. They were tiny men who wore bright caps and had long whiskers. And they were tired and hungry after a long day's work in the diamond mine.

"Look!" cried one. "Someone is sleeping on our beds!"

They touched Snow White's shoulder and she awoke with a start.

"Who are you?" the Dwarfs asked suspiciously.

When Snow White had told her sad story, the Dwarfs took pity on her.

"Stay here," one of them suggested. "You'll be safe with us."

"Can you bake apple tarts?" another Dwarf asked hopefully.

"Oh, yes! I can bake almost anything!" she laughed.

"We really like apple tarts," the Dwarfs told her.

SO IT was agreed that Snow White would take refuge in the cottage of the Seven Dwarfs. They mined the diamonds and she cooked their meals and in the evenings they shared amusing stories.

But the Dwarfs worried that the Queen's spies might still be looking for Snow White.

"Don't speak to any strangers while we're at work," they warned. "And don't open the door to anyone!"

"I'll be careful," she promised.

And so the months went by and Snow White grew even more beautiful. She read books and spent happy hours stitching her needlepoint. Sometimes she sang sweetly to herself and dreamed of marrying a handsome prince one day.

MEANWHILE, the wicked Queen believed Snow White was dead, and had stopped pestering the Mirror. But one morning she felt a little out of sorts and decided the Mirror could cheer her up.

"Am I not the fairest in all the land?" she asked the Mirror proudly.

"No, you are not the fairest," the Mirror replied. "Snow White is still the fairest."

"Snow White is dead!" cried the Queen.

"No, she isn't. She lives in the forest with the Seven Dwarfs," replied the Mirror.

The Queen shook with an icy fury. She called for her huntsman but was told he had fled the castle. So she plotted how she would destroy the princess once and for all!

SNOW WHITE was baking pies in the cottage when an old woman approached. It was the Wicked Queen, disguised in rags.

"I see you are baking apple tarts," the Wicked Queen commented through the open window.

"Yes," Snow White replied nervously. "I'm terribly sorry, but I can't speak to strangers."

"Oh, that's all right," the Queen replied. "I was just passing by and I'd like to leave you an apple. I sell them to make my living. Perhaps one day you'll buy some. They are the most delicious apples in the world."

The Wicked Queen cut a small piece of the apple with a knife and popped it into her mouth.

"See? The apple cannot harm you, child. Enjoy it." And she left quietly.

SNOW WHITE stared at the apple on the window ledge. It looked harmless. More than that, it shone and seemed so juicy that it was quite irresistible.

"It can't be poison," thought Snow White. "Why, the woman herself ate some."

Poor Snow White was wrong. The Wicked Queen had skillfully poisoned half the apple and had eaten the safe part.

No sooner had Snow White bitten into the fruit, than the blood drained from her cheeks and she collapsed onto the floor. And there she remained until the Dwarfs came home and found her.

"It must be the work of the wicked Queen!" they cried and tried everything they could to revive Snow White.

But she lay motionless and not one breath came from her lips to cloud a tiny mirror that they held up to her mouth.

THE Dwarfs wept bitterly for Snow White, unable to believe that she was really dead. In fact, as they gazed upon her, it seemed that she was only sleeping. Perhaps, they thought, she was under a spell and not truly dead. So they placed her in a glass-topped coffin and took turns guarding her.

It so happened that a young Prince from a nearby town heard about the beautiful young princess who lay in a glass coffin.

"I should like to pay my respects," he thought, and searched the forest until he found the house of the Seven Dwarfs.

As the Prince approached Snow White, he decided she was more beautiful than anyone he had ever seen.

"Please let me guard her!" he begged the Dwarfs. "I will protect her while she sleeps as long as I live. I can keep her safe from all harm."

At first the Dwarfs refused, but eventually they agreed their beloved Snow White might be safer at the Prince's castle.

As the Prince's men lifted the coffin, one of them tripped and the coffin was shaken.

Out popped the piece of poisoned apple from Snow White's throat! Her cheeks turned from ashen to rose and her eyes slowly fluttered open. The Dwarfs cheered while the Prince knelt beside Snow White, head bowed.

"I would like with all my heart for you to be my wife," the Prince whispered.

SNOW WHITE looked at the handsome Prince and her heart melted with love. "I will marry you," she said.

There was much celebrating and forgiving. Even the Wicked Queen was invited to the royal wedding. But the moment she saw Snow White's beauty and sweetness, she was so filled with hate and rage that she choked and died right on the spot!

As for Snow White and her Prince, they lived happily ever after in his castle, and the Seven Dwarfs never had to work in the diamond mines again.

HANSEL AND GRETEL

ONCE upon a time, there was a poor woodcutter who lived with his wife and two children, Hansel and Gretel. Times were so hard that the family had almost no food left.

One night the woodcutter cried in despair to his wife, "What shall we do? The children are surely going to starve to death."

"We must take them deep into the forest and leave them there," his wife answered sadly. "We must have hope that someone will find them and look after them."

The woodcutter nodded in agreement, his eyes brimming with tears. Heartbroken, the couple held each other tight and said no more.

Hansel and Gretel overheard their parents because hunger kept them awake. Gretel wept bitterly, but Hansel had an idea.

"Don't cry, Gretel," he smiled.

AFTER his parents had gone to sleep, Hansel quietly slipped out through the cottage door and gathered up dozens of white pebbles that shone as bright as silver dollars on the hard ground. Then he went back inside to bed.

THE NEXT morning, the father announced they were all going into the forest for firewood.

"Here is your bread for lunch," said their mother. "Eat it slowly. It's all you have for the day." Gretel tucked the bread into her apron because Hansel's pockets were full of pebbles.

As Hansel followed his parents into the forest, he dropped a pebble every few steps to mark the path.

The woodcutter built a fire for the children and told them to wait until he came back for them. Then he and his wife walked further into the forest. Hansel thought he heard them chopping wood nearby. But it was only the hollow sound of a woodpecker.

HANSEL and Gretel soon finished their bits of bread and slept until the fire burned out. The forest grew dark and Gretel became frightened.

"Don't worry, Gretel," Hansel said, and took his sister's hand.

As the moon rose high above them, Hansel found his shiny pebble path and they followed it back home.

Their parents seemed relieved to see them, but a few days later Gretel heard her mother say, "We have no food left at all. This time the children will have to go for good."

Hansel tried to find more pebbles, but this time the cottage door was locked tight.

AGAIN the parents led the children away with only small crusts of bread. Hansel broke his bread into little crumbs to scatter on the ground. The children were left with a fire to warm them as before and once again the parents walked away.

When the moon had risen, Hansel searched for his breadcrumb path. But the path was gone! The hungry forest birds had eaten every last crumb.

Hansel and Gretel shivered with cold and hunger. They saw a million eyes in the trees and imagined hungry teeth! Terrible noises and horrible shadows drew closer and closer!

The children held tightly to one another and soon cried themselves to sleep.

THE NEXT morning at first light, the children tried to find a way home.

"We keep going in circles," Hansel complained.

"And I'm so hungry," Gretel cried, "that I hardly have any strength left."

Soon they heard a beautiful songbird and followed it as it flew ahead of them. After a while, it led them to a clearing in the dense forest.

"DO YOU see what I see?" Gretel exclaimed, clapping her hands together. In the middle of the clearing was a gingerbread house with an almond paste roof and sugar windowpanes. Every flower in the garden was made of butter cream and there was a candy fence around the yard.

"Look!" Hansel cried. "Cookie shutters and real candy-canes and lemon drops!"

"The gingerbread is soft and fresh!" Gretel cried.

They didn't say another word but got busy breaking off pieces to eat.

"THE ROOF is delicious," Hansel declared between gulps and swallows. Gretel only nodded, eating some flowers, her mouth drenched in butter cream and icing sugar.

"Nibble, nibble little mouse, who's nibbling at my little house?" a tiny voice asked from behind closed shutters.

HANSEL and Gretel didn't bother to reply, they were too hungry. Soon, a little old woman, leaning on a cane, appeared in the doorway. "Children, my poor little children, do come in!"

And she brought them inside and fed them roast goose with apple stuffing and put them in a beautiful bedroom with fresh white sheets and huge feather pillows. The children sank gratefully into a sweet and deep sleep.

BUT THE next morning before Hansel had wakened, the little old lady pulled him quickly from his bed and pushed him into a wooden cage. She slammed the door and locked him in. Then she grabbed Gretel.

"Wake up, lazybones!" she shouted, "I like to roast little boys and you're going to help me fatten up your brother. You're also going to make the beds and clean my house!"

GRETEL was terrified when she realized that the old woman was not what she seemed.

"She must be a witch," Gretel thought in terrible dread.

Day after day, Gretel had to help the Witch make large dinners and pastries for Hansel to eat.

And at the end of each day, the Witch made Hansel stick out his finger to see how fat he was becoming. But Hansel knew the Witch couldn't see very well, so he fooled her and stuck out a skinny chicken bone instead.

Finally, the Witch flew into a rage. "You're not getting any fatter! I won't wait forever, you know!" she screamed.

THE NEXT morning after Gretel had washed the breakfast dishes, the Witch said, "Help me bake some pies, girlie. Today's the big day." And she cackled with a horrible mean sound.

The Witch built a roaring fire in the oven and when it was very hot, she said, "Crawl in and tell me if the flames are ready for our pies."

But Gretel suspected the Witch really wanted to eat her as an appetizer before Hansel.

"I'M TOO big," Gretel said bravely. "I can't fit into that oven."

"Don't be so stupid!" the Witch yelled. "Look, I can do it and I'm bigger than you."

And she leaned inside the oven to show Gretel. But Gretel pushed her as hard as she could and trapped the Witch inside the flames. She slammed the oven door tightly and that was the end of the Witch forever.

"HANSEL, we're free!" Gretel cried as she unlocked his cage. They packed as much food as they could carry into baskets. Under the Witch's bed they found a huge chocolate egg which broke open to reveal hundreds of diamonds, rubies and emeralds! The children stuffed them into their pockets.

This time they found their way home on the first try, and their parents cried tears of shame and relief.

"Can you ever forgive us for losing faith?" they asked.

"Oh yes!" Hansel and Gretel replied, and hugged them.

Then they showed the woodcutter all the wondrous things they'd brought home, and after that the family never needed for anything again.

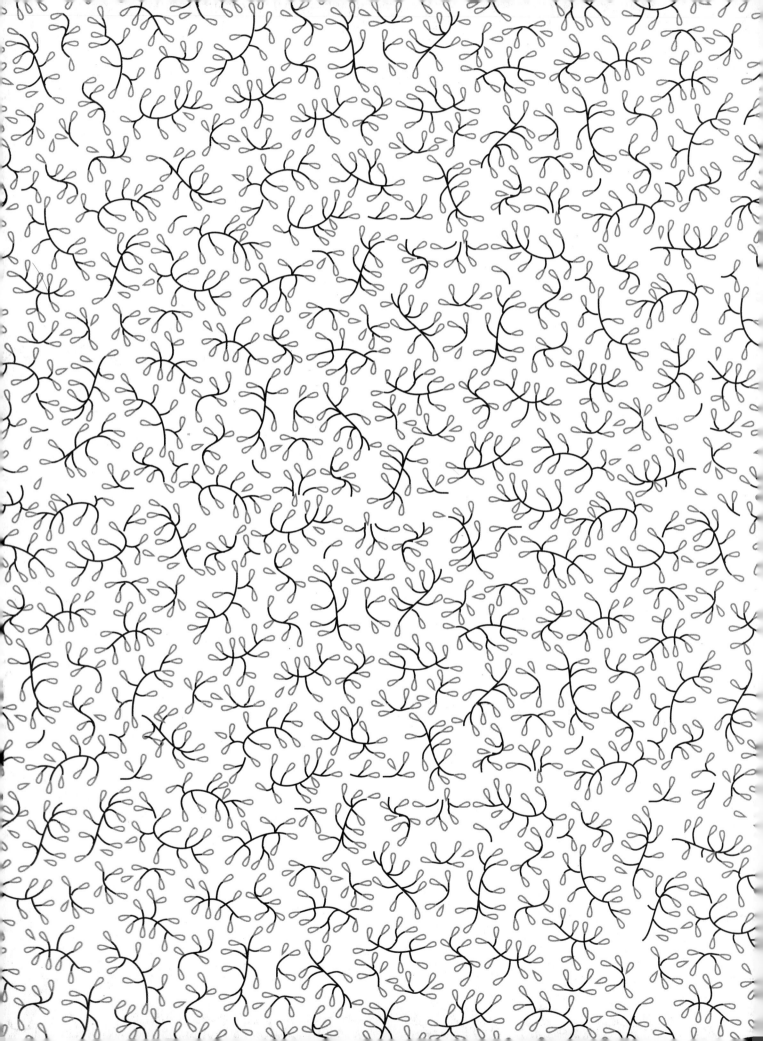